TREE-
HOUSE
COMIX
PROUDLY
PRESENTS

DOG MAN
LORD of the FLEAS

WRITTEN AND ILLUSTRATED BY **DAV PILKEY**

AS GEORGE BEARD AND HAROLD HUTCHINS

WITH COLOR BY JOSE GARIBALDI

graphix

AN IMPRINT OF

SCHOLASTIC

THANK YOU TO A DEAR FRIEND, RACHEL "RAY RAY" COUN, WHO WAS THERE FROM THE START

Library of Congress Control Number 2017963497

978-93-5275-595-0

Printed in India
First edition, September 2018
This edition April 2022

Edited by Anamika Bhatnagar
Book design by Dav Pilkey and Phil Falco
Color by Jose Garibaldi
Creative Director: David Saylor

CHAPTERS

DOG MAN
BeHind the Epicness!

Yo, Homies, It's George and Harold again!

What up, dogs?

We're in 5th grade now, which means we're totally mature.

And deep!

I think I might grow a moustache!

me too!

SQUEAK SQUEAK SQUEAK

AWESOME!

But--- our deepness and maturishness comes with a high price tag.

Our new teacher makes us read **CLASSIC LITERATURE!**

Fortunately, the books have all been pretty good.

Don't you agree, Harold?

Well, um...

I didn't really finish Lord of the Flies.

WHAT?

But don't worry! I've seen all the movies a bunch of times!!!

ALL **WHAT** movies?

You know: "**my Precious!**"

Well **I** read it, and it inspired me to write a new DOG man novel!

It's a story of savagery...

... a tale of consequences...

...A Profound Look into the constructs of morality...

... And one ring to rule them all!

SLAP!

But First, a recap of our Story thus far...

OUR STORY THUS FAR...

by George and Harold

One time there was a cop and a police dog...

...Who got hurt in an explosion.

KA-BLAMMERS

When they got to the hospital, the doctor had sad news:

BOO HOO

I'm sorry, but your body is dying.

And your head is dying, too, cop!!!

Rats!!!

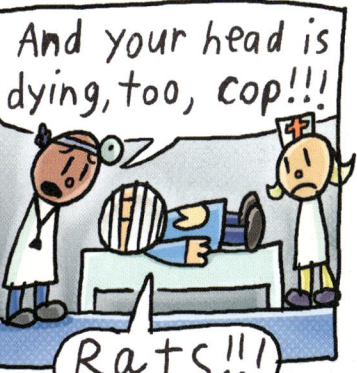

But just when everything seemed hopeless, the nurse Lady got an idea.

Let's sew the dog's head onto the cop's body!

OK, nurse Lady!

So they did.

And soon, a new crime-fighting sensation was unleashed.

HOORAY FOR DOG MAN!

Along the way, Dog Man has made some very awesome friends.

And one supa evil enemy!

WANTED
for being a jerk

PETEY
world's most evilest cat

Recently, Petey tried to clone himself...

I'll make a big, evil villain, just like me!

...but instead, he got a tiny, cute kitten who was <u>nothing</u> like him.

Papa!

Li'L Petey: world's Greatest kitty

Li'l Petey's Life started out Sad...

Free Kitty

...but it wasn't Sad for long.

Now Li'l Petey has a family.

80-HD: world's Greatest Robot buddy

And that is a good place to start.

Tree-
House
CoMix
Proudly
Presents

CHAPTER 1

A Visit from Kitty Protective Services

DOG Man

By George and Harold

One morning at Dog Man's house...

Buzz
Buzz
Buzz

DOG Man

clank
cLank
clank

...Li'L Petey and 80-HD were hard at work.

Buzz
Buzz
Buzz

clank
clank
clank

Well, I'm all done reprogramming the Dogmobile!

Now it's super easy to control!

How's the hydraulic Roof Ramp coming along?

14

CLUNK!

15

Grand Ballroom

♪*Ding*

Good morning, Dog Man!!!

Look what me and 80-HD did!

We transformed the Grand Ballroom into the coolest clubhouse **EVER!!!**

Us three are going to be in a club, ok?

We'll call ourselves the **SUPA BuDDieS!**

Most of the time, we'll just be our regular selves...

...But when danger rears its ugly head...

...We'll be super-heroes!!!

Look—I even made a cape for 80-HD!

And I made him a Flip-o-Rama mask!

FLIP FLOP FLIP

18

STEP 1.

First, place your left hand inside the dotted lines marked "Left hand here." Hold the book open FLAT!

STEP 2:

Grasp the right-hand page with your thumb and index finger (inside the dotted lines marked "Right Thumb Here").

STEP 3:

Now QUICKLY flip the right-hand page back and forth until the picture appears to be Animated.

(For extra fun, try adding your own sound-effects!)

.RAMA

Remember,

while you are flipping,
be sure you can see
the image on page 23
AND the image on page 25.

If you flip quickly,
the two pictures will
start to look like
one **Animated** cartoon!

Don't forget to
add your own
sound-effects!

Left
hand here.

Right
Thumb
here.

29

I'll go to School...

...and we can play together when I get back, okay?

Bye, Dog Man!
Bye, 80-HD!

33

Hey, where's the School at, Papa?

We're not going to School. We're getting outta town!

why?

Because you're in terrible **DANGER!**

why?

I'm not gonna tell you!

why?

Because every time I tell a Story, you always interrupt me, like, a Thousand Times!

why?

BECAUSE You're A PEST!!!

Why?

SiT DOWN!!!

why?

Because we need to talk!

why?

Look --- it's **very irritating** when you

Hey Papa, you got weird hairs in your nose!

YOU JUST INTERRU

I won't interrupt anymore. I'll be good.

ALRight, because what I'm about to tell you is

Hey Papa, is this story gonna be boring?

CHAPTER 2
PETEY'S STORY
WITH MANY (INTERRUPTIONS)

40

ALRIGHT! ALRIGHT!

I guess it all started when I was a kitten.

I used to be in the Critter Scouts!

Hey Papa, how come I'm wearing a hat?

That's NOT **You**! That's **ME** when I was a kitten!

Oh.

46

48

59

JUST PAY ATTENTION!

Okay.

So Anyway...

...Then, we're gonna take over the world in our **GIANT ROBO-BRONTOSAURUS!!!**

It's Parked outside!!!

HAW HAW HAW HAW HAW

HAW HAW HAW HAW HAW

63

65

So **THAT'S** why I came to get you...

...And **THAT'S** why we need to get as far away from here as possible.

But Papa, if the bad guys got locked up, why are we running?

Because they'll probably **ESCAPE**!

But how could they escape from a maximum security prison?

Who knows? Maybe something **DUMB** will happen!

Tree-House Comix Proudly Presents

Chapter 3

SomeThing DumB HappenS!

by George Beard and Harold Hutchins

69

Ten Minutes Later

Hello, I'm Sarah Hatoff reporting from Cat Jail...

...where chief and Milly have just caught three crooks!

How'd ya do it?

Well, first they attacked us...

Let's roll the clip...

...iN FLiP-O-RAMA

Left hand here.

Right
Thumb
here.

Things were looking bad for us...

...So we ran to the Jail Library...

...and fought back using the **Power** of **Books!**

Let's BOOK These Bozos!

OK, roll the clip!

FLIP-O-RAMA

Left hand here.

Right
Thumb
here.

82

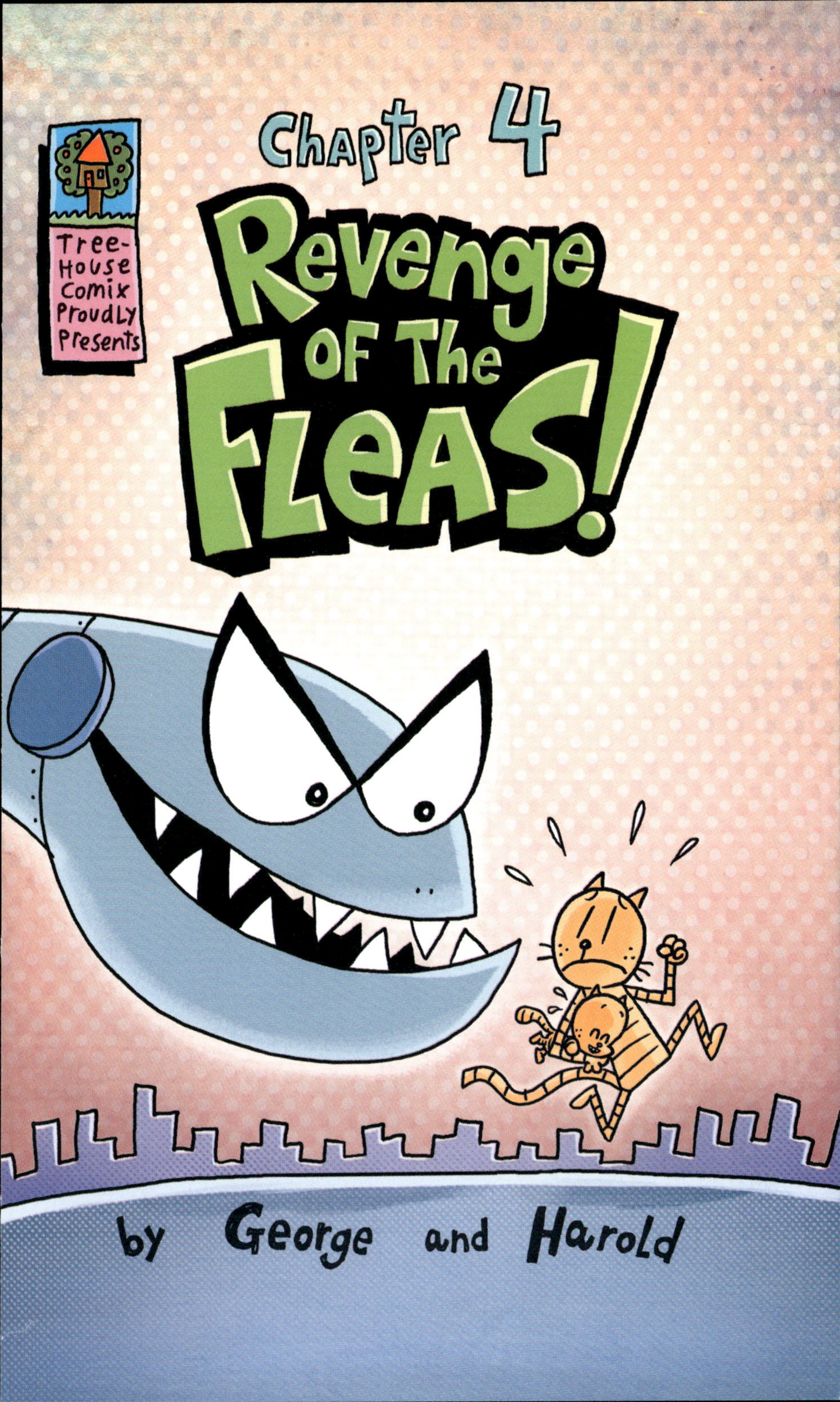

Chapter 4

Revenge OF THE FLEAS!

by George and Harold

87

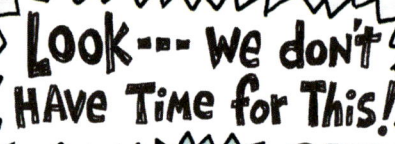

91

Left hand here.

Right
Thumb
here.

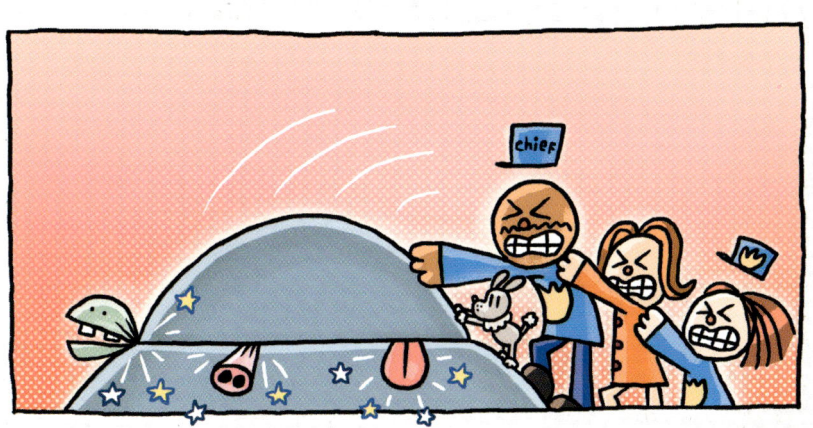

A Ladder Pooped on your head.

Ha Ha Ha Ha Ha Ha

A Ladder who?

A Ladder.

Uhhh...

Chapter 5
A Buncha Stuff That Happened Next

We now return with a breaking news update...

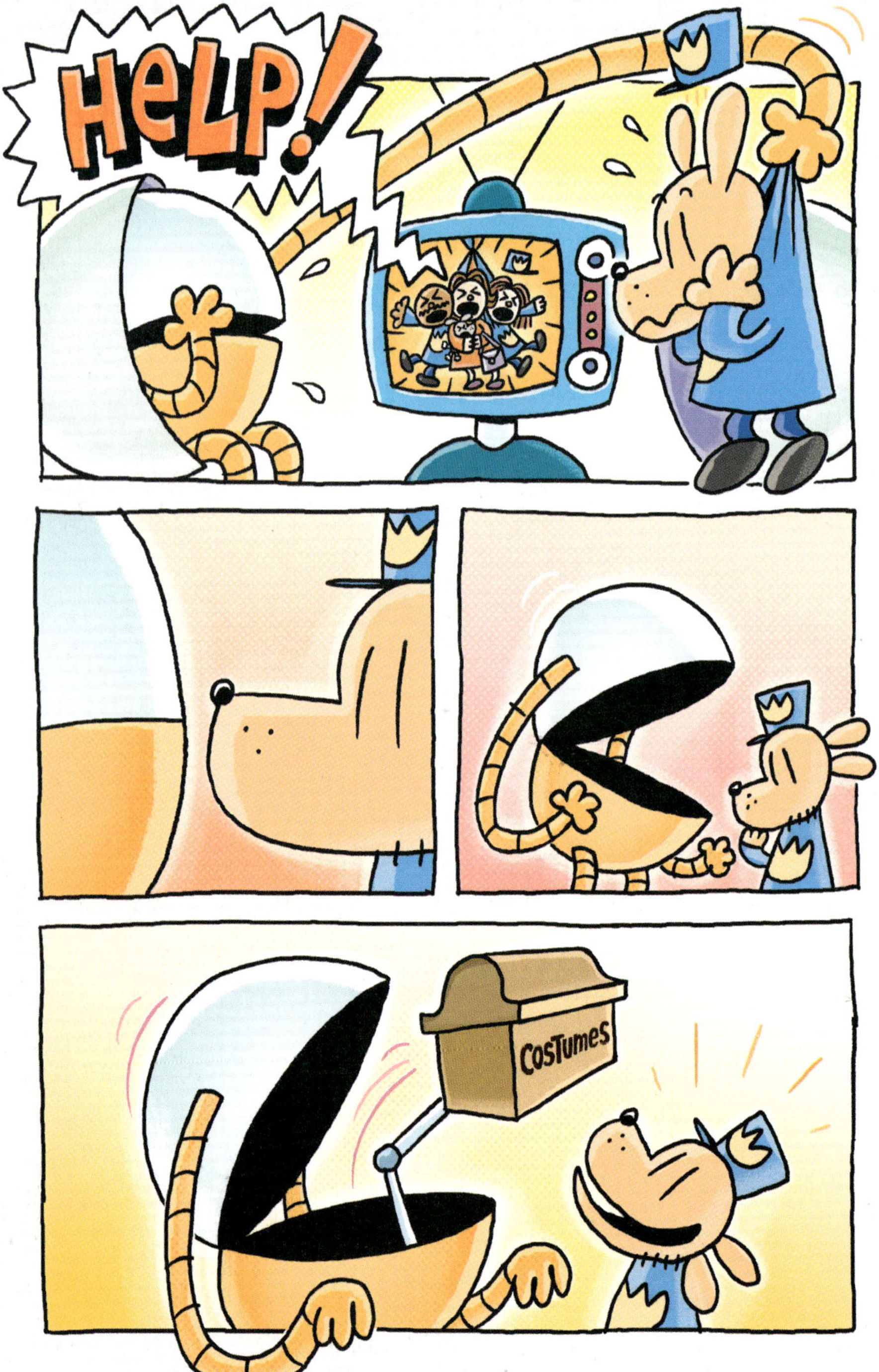

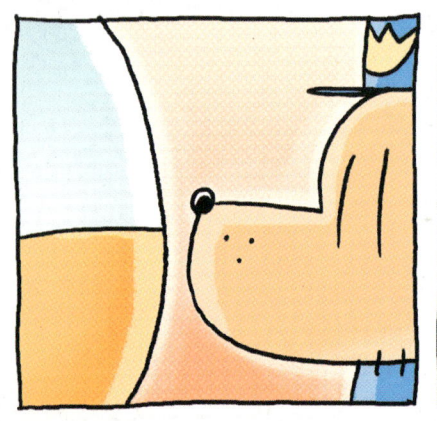

FLOOOP!

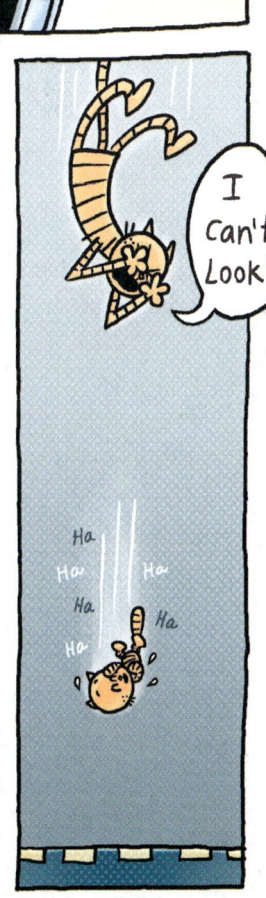

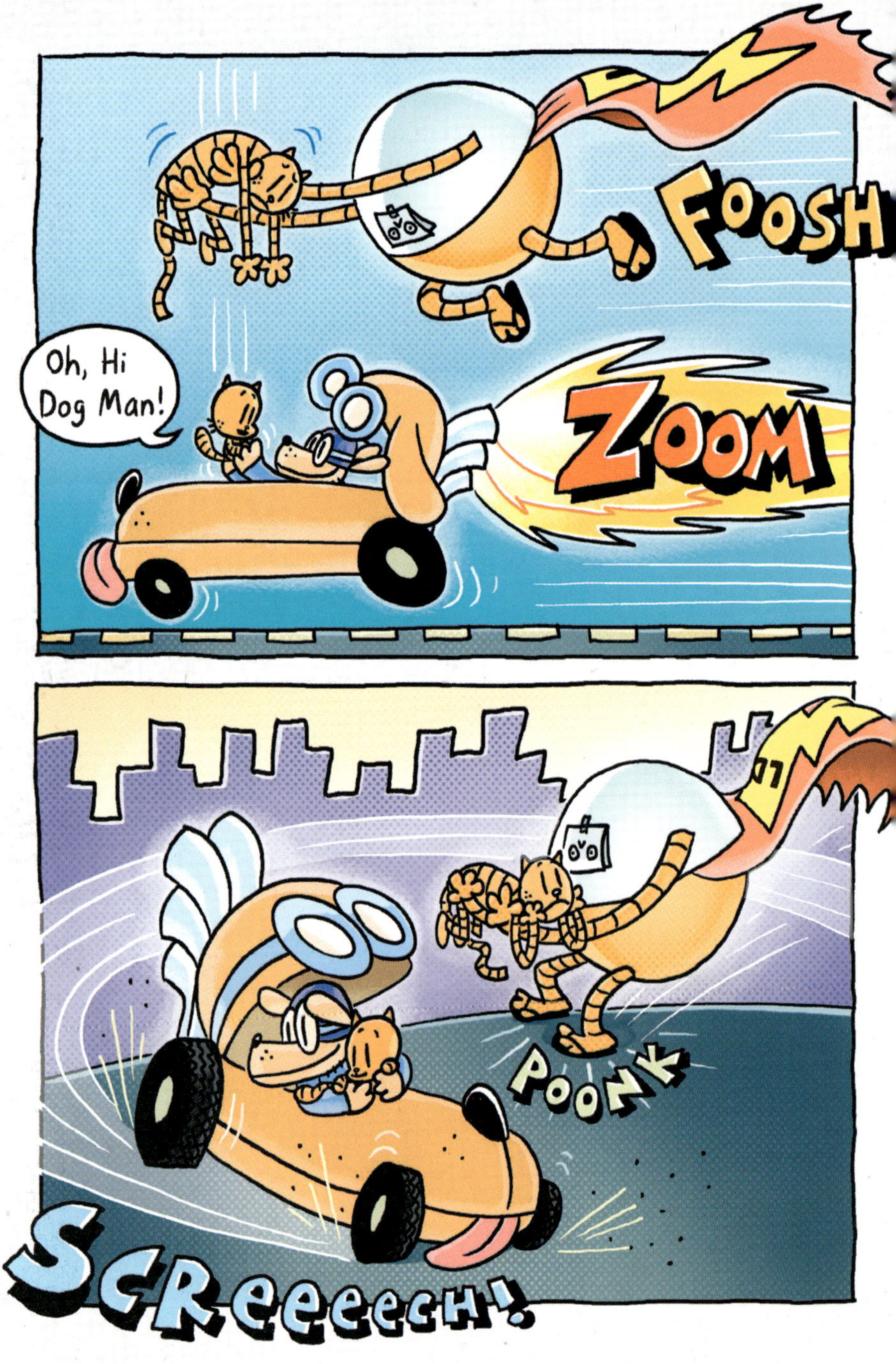
FOOSH
Oh, Hi Dog Man!
ZOOM
POONK
SCREEEECH!

CHAPTER 6

SUPA BUDDIES

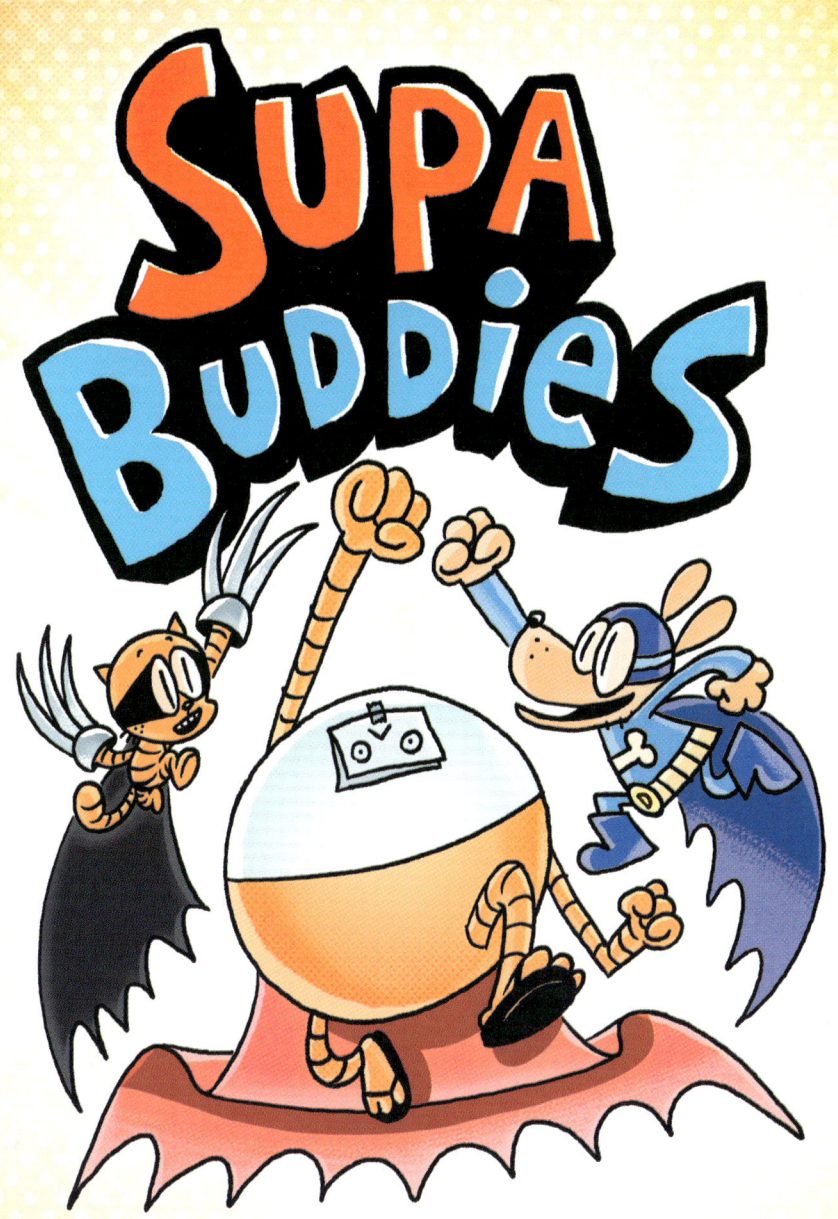

132

133

134

THAT'S **NOT** FUNNY!!!

138

144

145

Well, when you think about it...

None of us existed for trillions of years **BEFORE** we were born...

..And we didn't seem to mind it then!

Yeah--- I didn't even notice!!!!!

True dat!

Let's not cry 'cuz we're Gonna die. Let's Laugh 'cuz we Got to **LiVe!!!**

Ha-Ha!

Yeah! Ha-Ha!

FACTORY

148

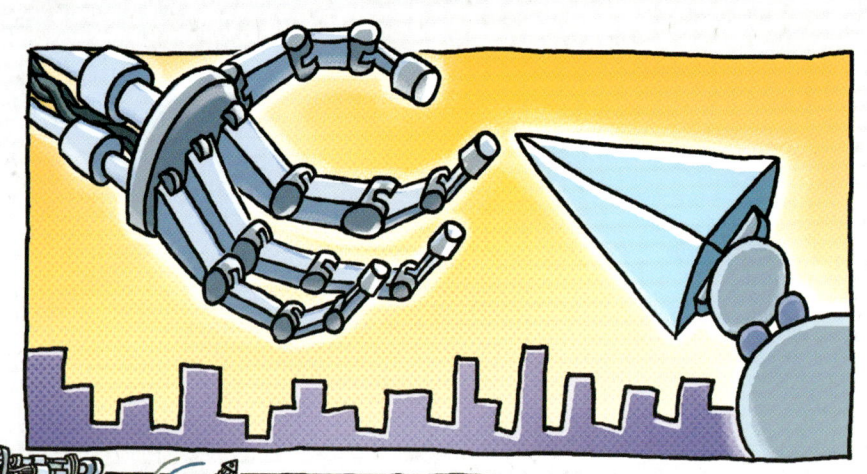

YANK!

Looks Like we're gonna have a Giant Robo-Battle...

...iN FLiP -O-RAMA!

Left hand here.

153

Right
Thumb
here.

155

Left hand here.

Right
Thumb
here.

Left hand here.

161

Right
Thumb
here.

CHAPTER 7
THE DARKNESS

Two hours Later...

PETEY!!!

CLONK

We've been battling for **HOURS**...

...And it hasn't gotten us **ANYWHERE!!!**

Haven't you always wanted a sidekick?

A Partner in crime?

Isn't that why you Created that dumb Little Kitten in the first place?

Fireflies give ya good Luck!

Let's go catch some more!!!

Oh, NO!!! Petey's in trouble! Let's GO!!

Well, well, Well...

All of my **Enemies** Are together in **ONE PLACE!** How **CONVENIENT!!!**

OH, *CRUNKY!* OH, **BUB!!!**

CRUNKY! BUB!!!

80-HD!!!

We gotta save Dog Man!!!

Oops! I mean, Lightning Dude!!!

We gotta save The Bark Knight!!!

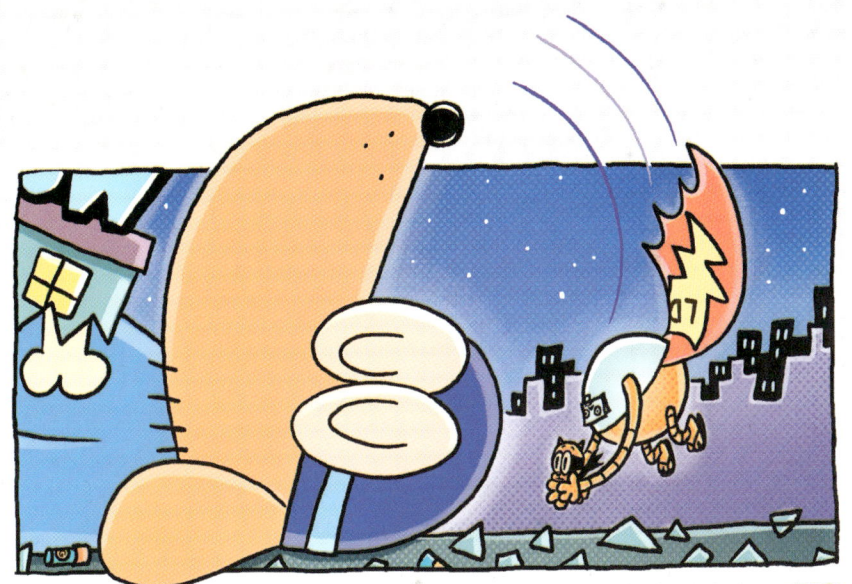

DOG MAN---
WAKE UP!!!

The Bad guys
Are Coming!!!

Well, well, well...
What do we have
here?

It Looks like you guys got yourselves in a big **Mess!!!**

Do you have any **LAST Words** before we **ZAP** you all to **SMiThereens?**

Ummm...

...hmmm...

We'll tell ya our last word in a minute, ok?

So, you've returned. Are you ready to tell us your final word?

Almost!

Shaka Shaka Shaka

OH, No! He's got Spray Paint!!!

CLOSE The hatch!!!

SSSSSSSSSSSSSS

SQUIRREL!

Left
hand here.

Right
Thumb
here.

203

205

Left
hand here.

Love, Sloppily

Right
Thumb
here.

Love, Sloppily

CHAPTER 8
MY DOG MAN HAS FLEAS!

Well, I guess we— hey, what's that?

What is it, Papa?

It's that Shrink ray I dropped back in chapter five.

Oh, yeah!

I wonder if it still works.

Let's find out!!!

ZAP

216

PETEY—YOU'RE BACK!

ka-click

Hey kid, y'wanna get some gelato with me after I escape tomorrow?

I don't know what gelato is, but okay!

Well, so long, Petey!

G'night, Chief!

... and desperately trying to figure out how to remove permanent marker from their faces before their moms find out!

So get ready for the next epic tale...

... of maturishness and deepality!!!

Because an all-new DOG MAN novel is coMing!!!

TREE-
HOUSE
COMIX
PROUDLY
Presents

DOG MAN
BRAWL of the WILD

IF You Like **THRILLS...**

...And you Like **LAFFS...**

...AND You Like **AWESOMENESS...**

...Then **DOG MAN is GO!**

"Dog Man is Go?"

That don't make no sense!

BUT We Like it!!!

The BARK KNIGHT

in **42** Ridiculously easy steps!

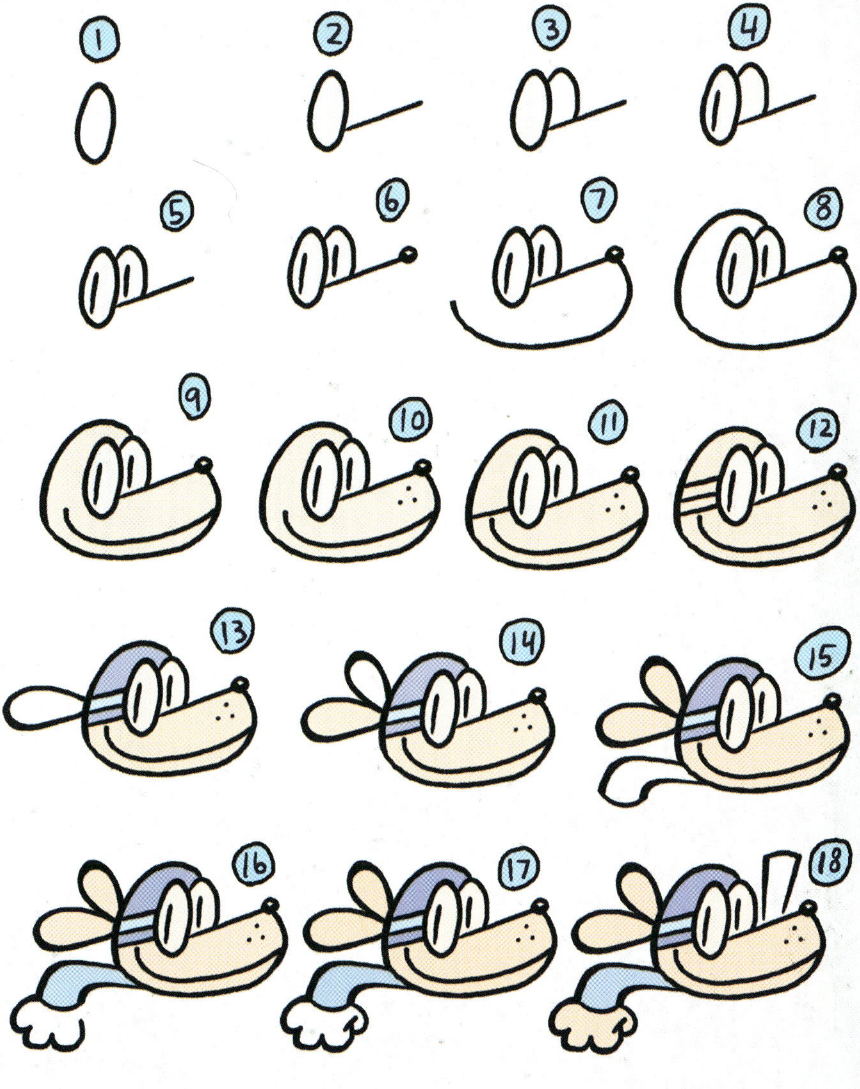

1
2
3
4
5
6
7
8
9
10
11
12
13
14
15
16
17
18

231

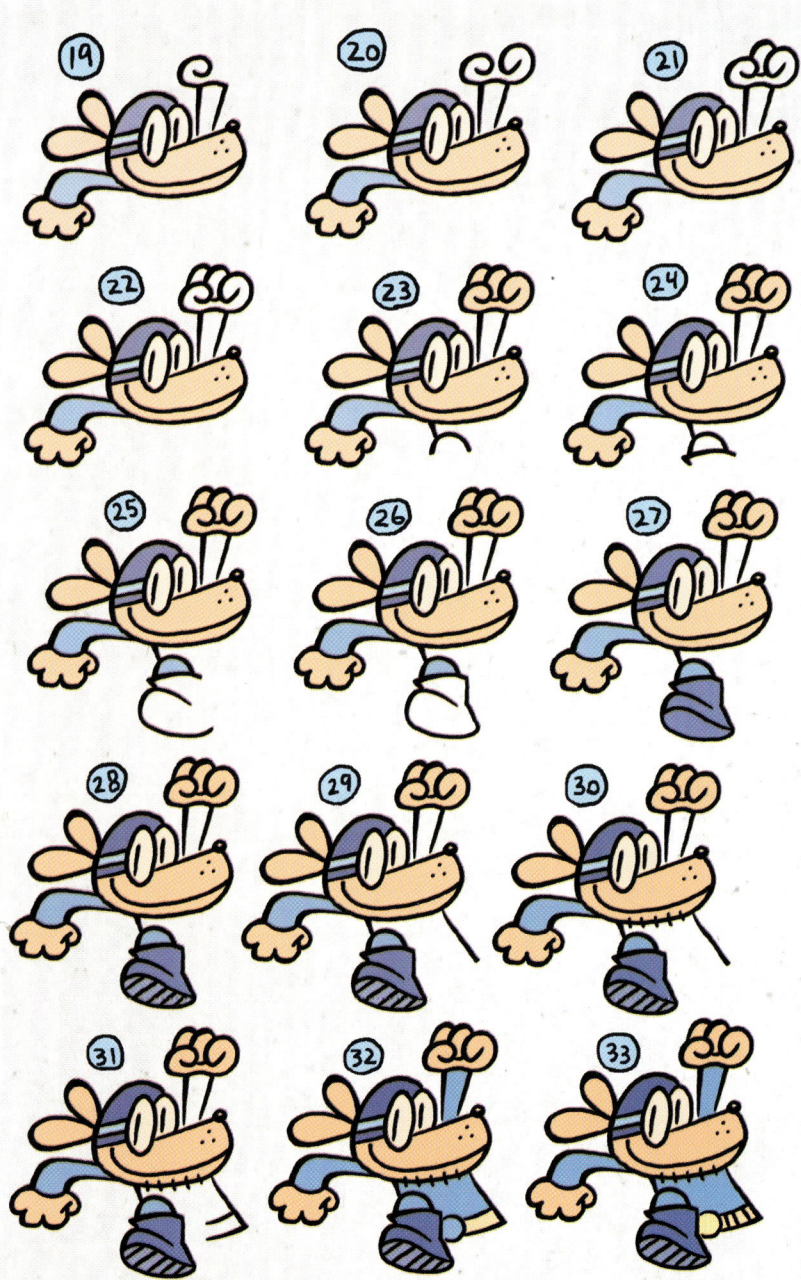

in **41** Ridiculously easy steps!

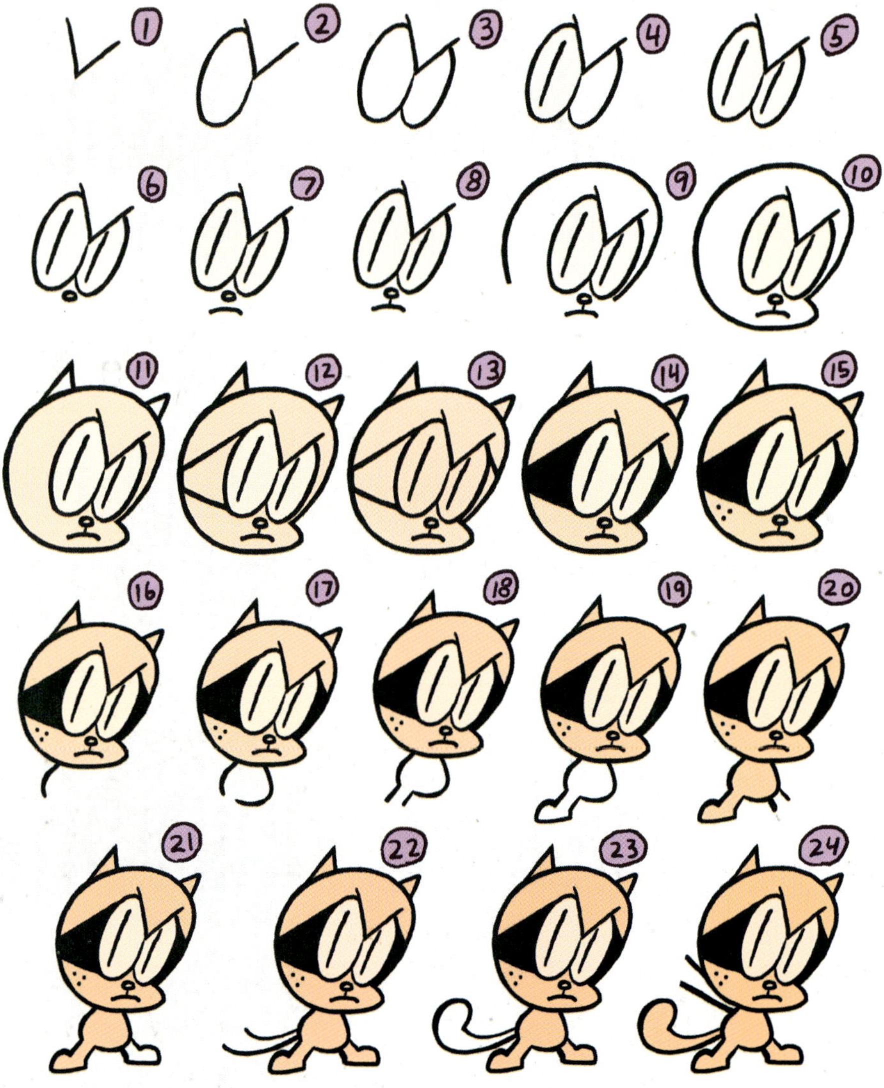

① ② ③ ④ ⑤

⑥ ⑦ ⑧ ⑨ ⑩

⑪ ⑫ ⑬ ⑭ ⑮

⑯ ⑰ ⑱ ⑲ ⑳

㉑ ㉒ ㉓ ㉔

234

235

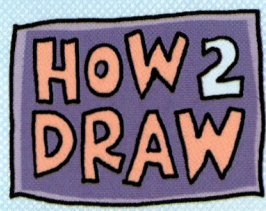

CRUNKY

in 26 Ridiculously easy steps!

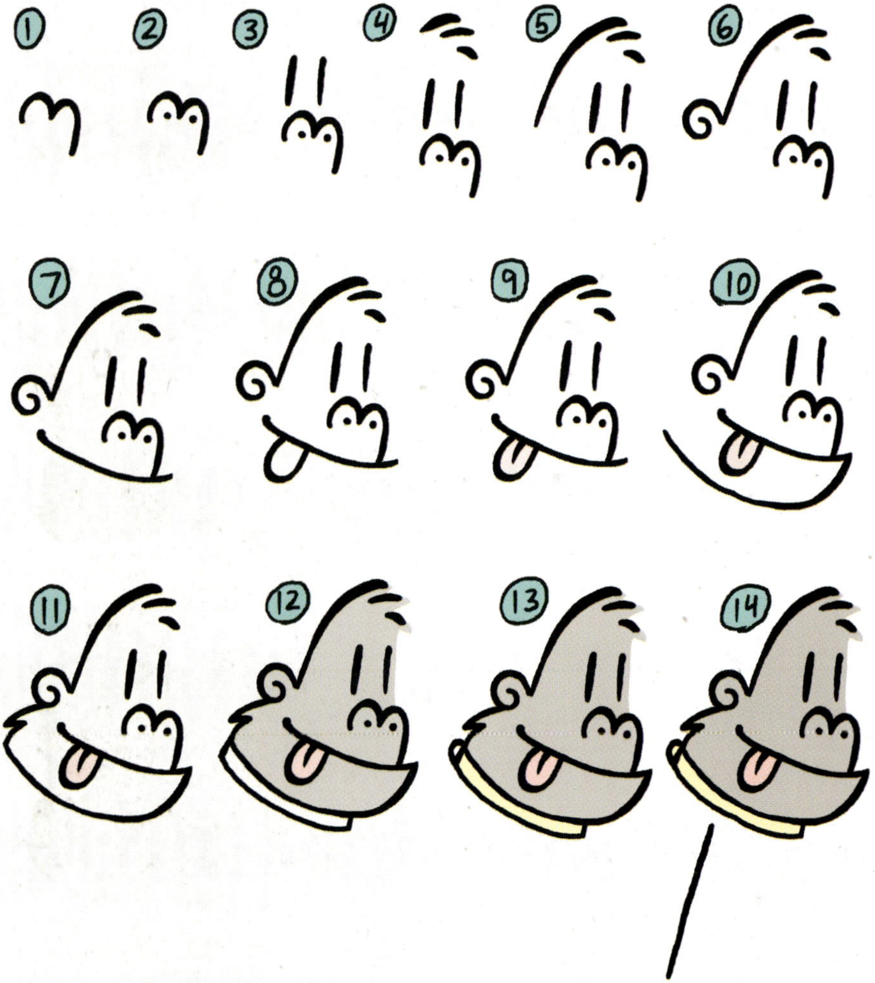

1

2

3

4

5

6

7

8

9

10

11

12

13

14

236

LiGHTNiNG DUDe ⚡LD

in **31** RidicuLously easy steps!

① ② ③ ④ ⑤ ⑥

⑦ ⑧ ⑨

⑩ ⑪ ⑫

⑬ ⑭ ⑮

⑯ ⑰ ⑱

238

PiGGY

in **33** Ridiculously easy steps!

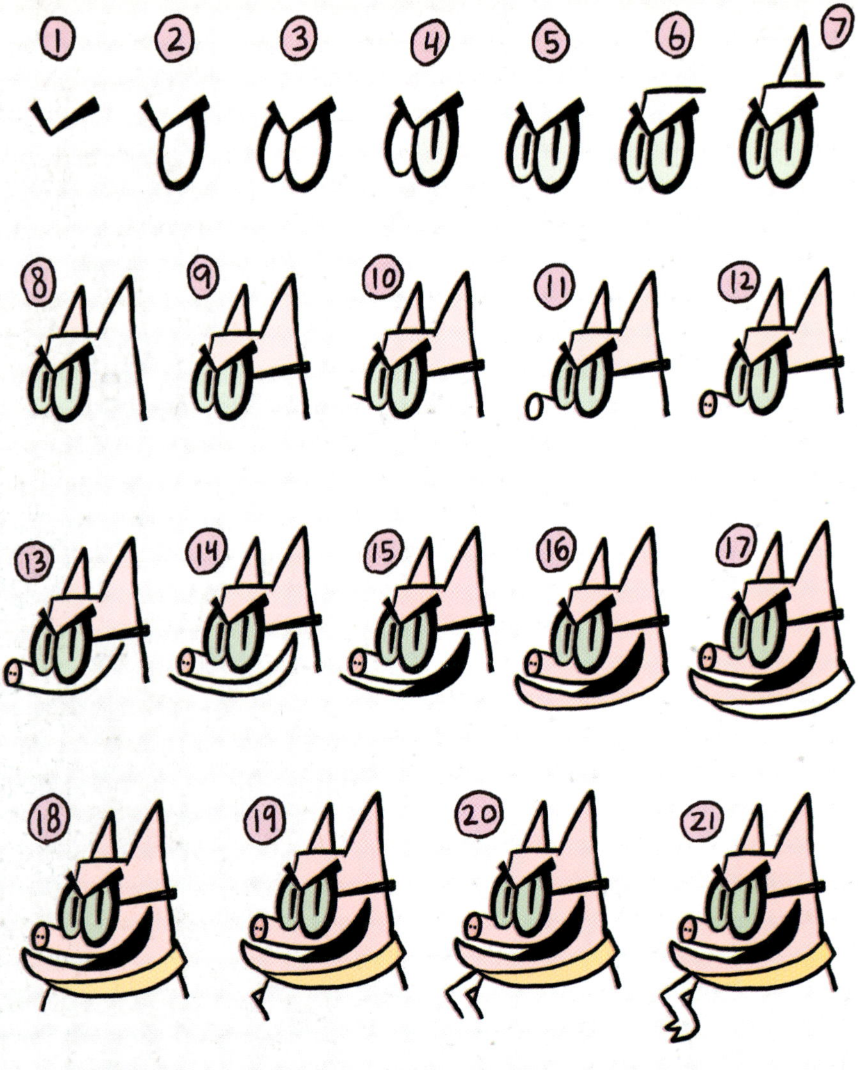

① ② ③ ④ ⑤ ⑥ ⑦

⑧ ⑨ ⑩ ⑪ ⑫

⑬ ⑭ ⑮ ⑯ ⑰

⑱ ⑲ ⑳ ㉑

240

in **21** Ridiculously easy steps!

242

Learn 2 Draw More STUFF!

at **ScholASTic.Com** and **Pilkey.com**

Notes

* accompanied by a parent or guardian

... and the cats get the benefits of human interaction and socialization.

This helps make it easier for shelter cats to get adopted!

It's a **Win-Win** for everybody!

Wow! That's a great idea, Papa!

cLick

check with
Your Local
animal shelter
and see if you
can volunteer to
READ To Your
CAT, KiD!

READING TO YOUR CAT IS ALWAYS A PAWS-ITIVE EXPERIENCE!

SOPHIE & SKIPPY

MAUDE & MAX

MAUDE & ABBY

MAX & ALEX

CHARLIE & PAPOOSA

#ReadtoyourcatkiD

AARON & PAPOOSA

JAC, KATE & DELILAH

KOUME, RINKA & YUMA

GALEN, FINN & RUCKUS

SOPHIA, ISABELLE, SCOOT & NINJA

LEARN MORE AT PILKEY.COM!

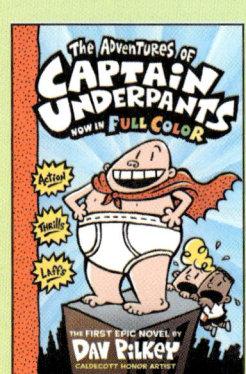

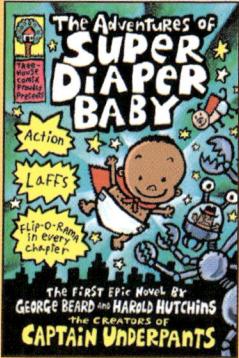 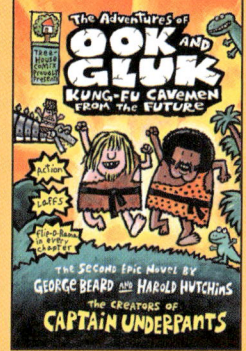 

ABOUT THE AUTHOR-ILLUSTRATOR

When Dav Pilkey was a kid, he suffered from ADHD, dyslexia, and behavioral problems. Dav was so disruptive in class that his teachers made him sit out in the hall every day. Luckily, Dav loved to draw and make up stories. He spent his time in the hallway creating his own original comic books.

In the second grade, Dav Pilkey created a comic book about a superhero named Captain Underpants. His teacher ripped it up and told him he couldn't spend the rest of his life making silly books.

Fortunately, Dav was not a very good listener.

ABOUT THE COLORIST

Jose Garibaldi grew up on the South Side of Chicago. As a kid, he was a daydreamer and a doodler, and now it's his full-time job to do both. Jose is a professional illustrator, painter, and cartoonist who has created work for Dark Horse Comics, Disney, Nickelodeon, MAD Magazine, and many more. He lives in Los Angeles, California, with his wife and their cats.